February Friend

Under the towel was a cage with a black-and-white rabbit inside. Torn newspapers covered the cage floor. A plastic water bottle hung from one side of the cage.

"There's a paper taped to the cage," Lucy said.

Mr. Vooray pulled the tape away. "It's a note," he said, unfolding the paper. He read it out loud: "THIS IS DOUGLAS. HE WANTS TO BE YOUR VALENTINE. PLEASE GIVE HIM A GOOD HOME. SIGNED, A FRIEND."

This book is dedicated to my February Friend, Zeke Roy
—**R.R.**

To Mark and Julia
—**J.S.G.**

Text copyright © 2009 by Ron Roy
Illustrations and map copyright © 2009 by John Steven Gurney

www.ronroy.com
www.randomhouse.com/kids

Educators and librarians, for a variety of teaching tools, visit us at
www.randomhouse.com/teachers

Library of Congress Cataloging-in-Publication Data
Roy, Ron.
February friend / by Ron Roy ; illustrated by John Steven Gurney.—1st ed.
    p.   cm. — (Calendar mysteries) "A Stepping Stone Book."
Summary: Bradley, Brian, Nate, and Lucy follow clues to find whoever left a rabbit in their first-grade classroom on Valentine's Day, because they are worried the rabbit will get sick and die of loneliness.
ISBN 978-0-375-85662-4 (trade) — ISBN 978-0-375-95662-1 (lib. bdg.)
[1. Mystery and detective stories. 2. Rabbits—Fiction. 3. Valentine's Day—Fiction. 4. Twins—Fiction. 5. Brothers and sisters—Fiction. 6. Cousins—Fiction.]
I. Gurney, John Steven, ill. II. Title.
PZ7.R8139Jan 2009 [Fic]—dc22   2008023906

Printed in the United States of America

10 9 8 7 6 5 4 3 2

Calendar MysTerieS

February Friend

by Ron Roy

illustrated by
John Steven Gurney

A STEPPING STONE BOOK™

Random House 🏠 New York

Contents

1. Secret Valentine 1

2. Who Left Douglas? 8

3. What's Wrong with Douglas? 13

4. Bad News 22

5. Running Out of Time 27

6. Scar Finger 33

7. Bunny in a Boat 37

8. Ellie to the Rescue 44

9. The Man with the Scar 50

10. Mystery Man 53

11. Bradley's Dream 58

12. A Perfect Plan 63

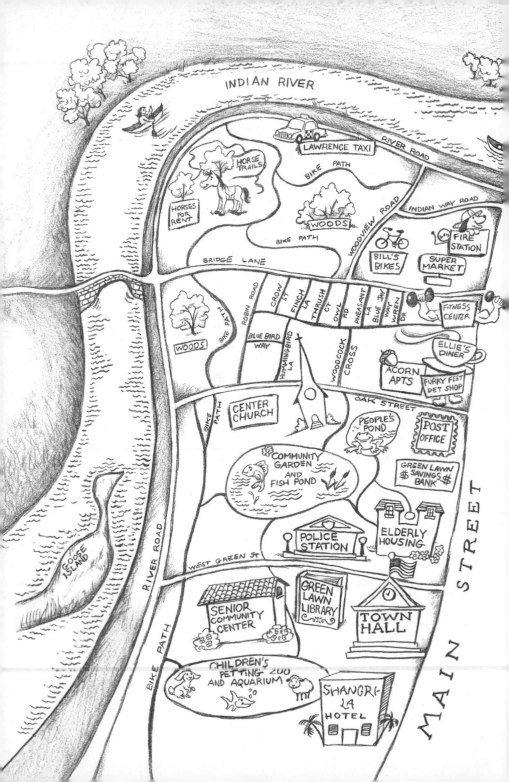

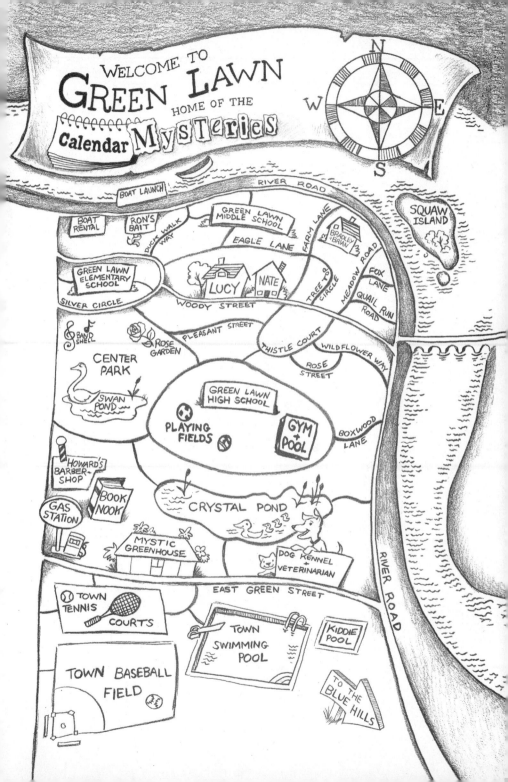

1
Secret Valentine

"I love Valentine's Day," Bradley Pinto told his twin brother. They were walking to school. Both boys had green caps pulled down over their red hair. They wore matching ski jackets.

"Why, because girls send you valentines?" Brian asked.

Bradley shook his head. "Nope. Because Mom always makes cupcakes!" He was carrying a box of them.

Bradley and Brian met their friends Nate Hathaway and Lucy Armstrong in front of their school. Nate had black hair like his older sister, Ruth Rose. Lucy's long blond ponytail hung from under her fuzzy white hat.

Lucy was staying with her cousin Dink's family for one year. Dink was best friends with Ruth Rose and the twins' brother, Josh. Lucy's parents were in Arizona helping to build a school on a reservation.

Nate tapped the box Bradley was holding. "How many cupcakes did your mom make?" he asked. He rubbed his tummy.

"Twenty-four," Bradley said.

"Is that all?" Nate asked. "I could eat ten all by myself!"

"Dream on," Lucy said.

Nate had brought paper plates, nap-kins, and plastic forks. Lucy was carry-ing a bag of heart-shaped candies.

Just then a loud bell clanged. The

four friends hurried into the school. A bunch of other kids were scurrying to their classrooms as well. A few parents came in carrying boxes. The janitor, Mr. Neater, was mopping up snow puddles.

The kids' first-grade teacher, Mr. Vooray, waited for them outside his classroom. The rest of the class was already in the room. Two of the kids were feeding Goldilocks, the hamster, and Yertle, the box turtle.

"Happy Valentine's Day," Mr. Vooray said. "Please put your goodies on the counter. And everyone hang up your coats."

Bradley, Nate, and Lucy carried the cupcakes, cookies, plates, and forks over to the counter. Bradley noticed other cupcakes, a plate of brownies, and a bowl of heart-shaped cookies.

A big red box sat on Mr. Vooray's desk. The box was decorated with paper hearts. All the kids knew it was filled with valentines. They had been making them all week.

"When can we open the box?" Samantha asked Mr. Vooray.

"As you know, today is a half day," Mr. Vooray said. "I think we should wait till just before we go home. Then we can pass out the valentines and eat all the treats you kids brought in."

The morning went quickly. The first graders did math problems. Then they wrote in their journals. When they were finished with that, they read in their library books.

Then Mr. Vooray read aloud from *Charlotte's Web.*

Suddenly Nate's tummy growled.

Mr. Vooray looked up. "I guess it's time to eat," he said with a smile.

Everyone jumped up and ran for the counter. Kids giggled and bumped into each other as they handed out paper plates, napkins, forks, and cups of juice. Then the kids who had brought food passed it out. Soon everyone was munching.

Bradley bit into a chocolate cupcake with pink frosting. He and his mom had frosted them early that morning.

"When can we get our valentines?" Joyce asked.

"Right now!" Mr. Vooray said. He pulled the lid off of the red box and dumped a big pile of valentine cards on his desk. He picked Flo, Bradley, and Lucy to pass them out to the class.

"Hey, Mr. Vooray, here's one with no name on it," Bradley said. He held up the envelope. It was red and shaped like a heart.

Mr. Vooray grinned. "It's a mystery card," he said.

"Open it!" a bunch of kids yelled.

"Go ahead," said Mr. Vooray.

Bradley opened the envelope. He pulled out a heart-shaped card and showed the class. On the front was a picture of a bunny rabbit.

Bradley read what was written inside the card: "LOOK IN THE CLOSET."

Mr. Vooray walked over to the closet. He put his ear to the door. "I hear something," he whispered.

2
Who Left Douglas?

"Should we look inside?" Mr. Vooray asked.

"Yes!" everyone yelled.

Mr. Vooray pulled the door open. "Well, what is this?" he asked.

Twenty kids jumped out of their seats and crowded behind Mr. Vooray.

Sitting on the closet floor was a square shape under a towel.

"Maybe it's more cupcakes," said Joyce.

Mr. Vooray gently removed the towel.

"Ooooh," said twenty voices.

Under the towel was a cage with a
black-and-white rabbit inside. Torn
newspapers covered the cage floor. A
plastic water bottle hung from one side
of the cage.

"How cute!" Tiffany said.

"There's a paper taped to the cage,"
Lucy said.

Mr. Vooray pulled the tape away. "It's a note," he said, unfolding the paper. He read it out loud: "THIS IS DOUGLAS. HE WANTS TO BE YOUR VALENTINE. PLEASE GIVE HIM A GOOD HOME. SIGNED, A FRIEND."

"Can we keep him?" asked Nate.

"Who left him here?" demanded Rodney.

"Douglas is a silly name for a rabbit!" announced Kaitlyn.

Bradley noticed a jar filled with brown pellets on the floor next to the cage. "Is that the rabbit's food?" he asked.

Mr. Vooray picked up the jar. "I think you're right, Bradley," he said.

"He eats that yucky stuff?" Brian asked. "Don't rabbits eat lettuce?"

"Good question, Brian," Mr. Vooray said. "Why don't you look it up and tell us when we come back on Tuesday?"

"Can we take him out of the cage?" Veronica asked.

"I don't think so," Mr. Vooray said. "Poor Douglas doesn't look happy."

The rabbit's eyes were closed. His ears didn't wiggle. His nose didn't twitch. Nothing on Douglas moved.

Bradley picked up the towel. "Look, there's a capital *Z* on it."

"Maybe it's a clue to who left Douglas!" Lucy said.

"You could be right," Mr. Vooray said. "Do we know anyone whose name begins with *Z*?"

"Zorro!" said Nate.

Everyone laughed.

"All right, let's take our seats, please," Mr. Vooray said.

Twenty kids scrambled back to their desks.

Mr. Vooray pointed to a sheet of paper tacked to the bulletin board. "Veronica, I see it's your turn to take Goldilocks home for the long weekend," he said. "Don't forget, Monday is a holi-day. It's Presidents' Day."

Veronica got up and brought the hamster cage to her seat.

"Good. Mikey, you're signed up to take Yertle," Mr. Vooray added.

Mikey put Yertle into his traveling box and carried the box to his desk.

"Now we need someone to take Douglas home," Mr. Vooray went on.

"I will!" Bradley said.

"Are you sure, Bradley?" Mr. Vooray asked. "Will this be okay with your parents?"

"They love animals," Bradley said. "We have a pony and a dog already!"

Mr. Vooray grinned. "Yes, I know. Okay, you and your brother can take Douglas home. On Tuesday we can decide what to do about this mystery."

3
What's Wrong with Douglas?

After school, Lucy and Nate went to the twins' house. Bradley and Brian each held an end of the cage as they walked home. The towel was draped over the cage so Douglas wouldn't get too cold. Lucy carried the jar of rabbit food.

"I wonder who left him in the closet," Nate said. "Maybe it was a kid in another grade."

"Why would a kid get rid of a rabbit?" Bradley asked.

Nate shrugged. "Maybe the kid's parents made him do it," he said.

"It had to be a kid or someone who works at the school," Brian said.

"Why?" Lucy asked.

"Who else could get into Mr. Vooray's classroom?" Brian asked.

"Bri, there were parents all over the building today," Bradley said. "Some of them came in to bring food and help with the parties."

"You're right," Lucy said. "Some kid's mom or dad could have left Douglas."

"Or what about the guy who brings the milk every day?" Bradley asked. "Or the woman who delivers the mail? And there was a plumber fixing a toilet in the boys' bathroom."

"In other words, it could be anyone," Nate said.

Ten minutes later, the kids trooped

into Bradley and Brian's kitchen.

Mrs. Pinto was sitting at the table, chopping vegetables. "Hi, kids. Leave your boots by the door, please," she said. The kids all removed their boots.

"Mom, we got a rabbit!" Bradley announced. He and Brian set the cage on the floor.

Brian whipped off the towel. "His name is Douglas, and we get to keep him for the long weekend!"

Mrs. Pinto walked over and peered into the cage. "Hello, Douglas," she said. Then she looked at her twin sons. "Where did you get him?"

They explained about the mystery valentine at school.

"How odd," Mrs. Pinto said.

The kids yanked off their hats and coats. They all knelt around the cage.

"Don't scare him!" Bradley said.

"We're not!" Brian said.

"Let's all just be quiet for a minute," their mother said. "Rabbits are timid animals."

They all watched Douglas in the cage. He huddled in a corner, not moving a whisker.

"He didn't move at school, either," Bradley said.

"Maybe he's hungry," Lucy said.

Mrs. Pinto grabbed a slice of carrot from her cutting board. She pushed it through the cage bars. Douglas didn't even look at it.

"What's the matter with him?" Brian asked his mother. "Is he sick?"

"I don't know," Mrs. Pinto said. "Maybe he's just scared."

Just then their dog, Pal, trotted into the kitchen. He stuck his nose up against the cage. "Woof!" he said.

Douglas ignored Pal.

Bradley petted his dog. "Douglas

isn't feeling good," he explained to Pal. "Can we keep Douglas in our room, Mom?"

"Sure," his mother said. "Maybe after a while he'll get more perky."

The four kids lugged the cage and jar of food up the stairs.

They bumped into Josh at the top of the stairs. Josh was Bradley and Brian's twelve-year-old brother.

"What's in the cage?" Josh asked.

"A rabbit," Brian said. "We're keeping him for the weekend."

"Cool," Josh said. He put his finger into the cage.

"His name is Douglas," Lucy told Josh. "But he may be sick. He won't move or anything."

Josh stared into the cage. "Maybe he's just taking a nap," he said. Then he headed downstairs.

The kids brought the cage into Bradley and Brian's room. They set it on Bradley's desk. Lucy filled the water bottle in the bathroom. Bradley put a handful of the rabbit food in the cage in front of Douglas's nose.

When Bradley took his hand away, he felt something smooth under the newspapers. "I found something," he said. He felt around under the papers and pulled out a Baggie. Inside the

Baggie were three photographs. Bradley laid them on his bed.

"They're pictures of Douglas," Lucy said.

The kids looked at the pictures.

In one, he was just a small bunny sitting in a man's hand.

Another picture showed Douglas in a yard somewhere.

In the third picture, Douglas was sitting on a wooden bench. There was water in the background.

"I wonder who took these pictures," Lucy said.

"Probably his owner," Bradley said.

"The mystery man!" Brian said in a spooky voice.

"I wonder if Douglas got left in the closet because he's sick," Lucy said. "That's a pretty mean thing to do!"

Bradley walked over to his bookshelf. He found a book about pets.

He turned to the chapter on rabbits. "Guys, listen to this," he said. "'If your pet rabbit stops eating, playing, or hopping around, he may be sick. Take him to a veterinarian immediately.'"

The four kids stared into the cage. Douglas sat as still as a stone.

"We have to take him to Dr. Henry," Bradley announced.

"Who's he?" Lucy asked.

"The vet," Nate explained. "My sister, Ruth Rose, brings our cat there. Doc Henry is real nice."

Bradley ran downstairs. "Mom, can you call Dr. Henry?" he asked. "Douglas still looks like he's sick."

The other kids came downstairs while Mrs. Pinto punched in the telephone number.

Bradley listened as his mother told the vet about the rabbit.

"Okay, thank you, Dr. Henry," said

Bradley's mother. Then she hung up.

"What did he say, Mom?" Bradley asked.

"If Douglas doesn't improve overnight, he'll take a look at him tomorrow," Bradley's mother said. "Don't worry, hon, Douglas will be fine."

But Bradley did worry. That night, he slept on the floor next to Douglas's cage.

4
Bad News

As soon as Bradley woke up Saturday morning, he peered into the cage. Douglas was sitting in a corner. He wasn't moving.

"Douglas," Bradley whispered, "are you all right?"

Bradley reached into the cage and put his hand on Douglas's back. The rabbit felt warm, and Bradley could tell that he was breathing. But that was all he was doing.

Bradley started to get dressed.

"What's going on?" Brian asked from his bed.

"Doc Henry told Mom to bring Douglas in if he didn't get better," Bradley reminded him. "And he didn't."

Brian sat up and blinked. "I'm coming, too," he said.

The boys got dressed, woke their mother, and made themselves cereal for breakfast.

Between spoonfuls, Brian called Nate. "We're taking Douglas to the vet," he said. "You want to come? Get Lucy, too."

When Nate and Lucy arrived, Mrs. Pinto drove them all to the vet's office on East Green Street. The four kids crowded into the office with the cage.

Dr. Henry was waiting. "So here's the mystery bunny," he said. "Let's take a look."

Dr. Henry gently lifted Douglas out of the cage. He placed the rabbit on his examination table.

Bradley noticed that Douglas was trembling. "Why is he shaking?" he asked.

"He's scared," Dr. Henry said.

The vet ran his hands all over Douglas's body. He looked inside his ears, eyes, and mouth. He weighed Douglas on a small scale and took his temperature. He parted Douglas's fur and studied his skin.

"Well, I'd say this is a very healthy rabbit," Dr. Henry stated. "His eyes are clear, and his teeth are perfect."

Bradley showed Dr. Henry the pellets he had in his pocket.

"These are a fine brand of rabbit food," the vet said. "Someone took very good care of this fellow."

"So what could be wrong with him?"

Bradley asked. "He won't move or anything."

"I've seen this before," the vet said. "Dogs, cats, even monkeys, sometimes stop eating when they feel lonely. I think your rabbit misses his owner. He feels abandoned, confused. He may be in shock, and that's why he won't eat or drink."

The kids looked at Douglas on the table.

Dr. Henry put the rabbit back into his cage. "I'm afraid Douglas will become very sick if he doesn't start eating and taking water," he said. "He could die."

"But what can we do?" Bradley asked.

Dr. Henry stroked the rabbit's soft ears. "If this were my rabbit, I'd return him to his real owner," he said. "And soon."

5
Running Out
of Time

On their way home, the twins' mom drove up Main Street. Brian sat up front and the other kids were in the back. Douglas's cage lay across their laps.

Suddenly Bradley sat up. He tapped his mother's shoulder. "Mom, stop!" he shouted.

"Here? Why?" his mother asked.

"I want to take Douglas into the pet shop," Bradley said. "Mrs. Wong might know his owner!"

"Great idea," his mother said. She pulled the car up in front of the Furry Feet Pet Shop. All four kids climbed out. Bradley and Lucy carried the cage through the front door.

"Hi, kids," Mrs. Wong said. "What have you got?"

Mrs. Wong was dropping fish food into an aquarium. All along the walls were fish tanks and animal cages.

"It's a rabbit, and he won't eat," Nate said.

Mrs. Wong peered into the cage at Douglas.

The kids explained how Douglas had been left in their classroom closet. Then they told her what Dr. Henry had told them.

"So you want to know if I know the owner, right?" Mrs. Wong asked.

The four kids nodded.

Mrs. Wong put her hand in the cage.

She stroked the rabbit's fur. Douglas sat in a corner with his eyes closed.

"I'm sorry, but I've never seen this bunny," she said. "And I don't know anyone in town who owns one like this."

Bradley felt awful. How would they ever find Douglas's owner?

The kids thanked Mrs. Wong and carried Douglas back to the car.

"Any luck?" Bradley's mom asked. She pulled into traffic.

"No, she'd never seen Douglas before," Bradley said.

"I'm sorry, hon," his mother said.

"I have an idea," Nate said. "We could put an ad in the newspaper. We could ask whoever left Douglas at the school to get in touch with us."

"But that could take days," Bradley said.

"We need to find Douglas's owner soon!" Lucy said.

When they got home, the kids carried Douglas back up to Bradley and Brian's room.

"Come down in a few minutes," the twins' mom called up the stairs. "I'll make hot chocolate."

"Thanks, Mom!" Brian yelled back.

They set the cage on Bradley's desk.

"He doesn't look any different," Nate said.

"Maybe we should leave him alone for a while," Lucy said.

"Maybe he just doesn't like kids," Brian suggested.

They all stared at the rabbit. His eyes were closed, and he didn't move.

"Come on," Bradley said sadly. "Let's go downstairs."

He picked up the three photos as they left the room.

Bradley's mom was stirring a pot of hot chocolate on the stove.

The kids sat and Bradley spread out the pictures of Douglas.

"Where'd you get those?" the twins' mother asked.

"They were in the cage," Brian said. "His owner must have left them."

Lucy pointed to the picture that showed Douglas in someone's hand. "He was so cute when he was little," she said.

Suddenly Bradley had an idea. "Guys, these pictures could be clues!" he said.

6
Scar Finger

"Clues to what?" Nate asked.

"We want to find Douglas's owner, right?" Bradley said. He pointed at the hand holding the tiny rabbit. "If this is his owner's hand, maybe we can find out who it is!"

They all stared at the picture.

Bradley's mother reached over and pointed with her mixing spoon. "Well, we can tell that it's a man's right hand," she said.

"Boy, he has hairy knuckles!" Nate said.

"And he's got a scar on his little finger," Lucy put in.

The kids bent closer to the picture. "The scar is shaped like the letter *C*," Bradley said.

"Cool," Nate said. "Now we just have to find a hairy guy with that scar on his right pinkie."

"Lots of luck," Brian said.

Lucy studied the picture showing Douglas on a patch of grass. "He must live somewhere with a lawn," she said. "And tall hedges."

"That's about half the yards in Green Lawn," Nate said. "Even *we* have hedges!"

Bradley took a closer look at the picture. "He grows vegetables," he said. "See, those are tomatoes."

Bradley's mother set four mugs and a bag of marshmallows on the table. "Careful, it's hot!" she said.

They thanked Mrs. Pinto and took noisy sips.

"Well, we'll never find the vegetable garden," Brian said. He pointed out the kitchen window. "There's a foot of snow in everyone's yard."

"What about other clues?" Lucy asked. She picked up the picture that showed Douglas sitting on the wooden bench. "Are there any benches like this in Green Lawn?"

Bradley studied the picture. "Guys, I don't think this is a bench," he said.

"Then what is it?" Brian asked, taking the picture.

"I think it's a seat in a rowboat," Bradley said. "See the water behind it? And that's not a railing, it's the outside of the boat."

Bradley opened a drawer under the counter. He pulled out a magnifying glass and held it over the picture. "It says

S-K-I on the side of the boat," he said.

Brian grinned. "Ron's Bait Shop has boats for rent," he said. "Ron's last name is Pinkowski, and people call him Ski."

"Awesome!" Nate said. "Let's go ask him if he knows anyone with a rabbit."

"It's February," Brian said. "Mr. Pinkowski rents out boats in the summertime."

Bradley shook his head. "He sells bait for ice fishing, too."

He grabbed the three pictures. "What are we waiting for?" he asked.

7
Bunny in a Boat

The kids hiked on River Road, along Indian River. The sun shone brightly on the snow and the water.

"How far is it to the bait shop?" Lucy asked.

"It's just up the river, past the middle school," Bradley said.

Soon they saw the bait shop. It was a small wooden building with windows facing the river. Smoke came from a chimney. A black pickup truck sat next to the shop.

"I hear a noise," Nate said.

They all did. *THWACK! THWACK! THWACK!*

The kids walked around the building to the entrance. A tall man with a beard was chopping wood. His nose was red and his breath was white.

"Hi, Mr. Pinkowski," Bradley said.

The man looked up and smiled. He set his ax down and wiped his face with a handkerchief. "Hi, kids." He smiled at Lucy. "Have we met?"

"This is Lucy," Bradley said. "She's Dink's cousin from California."

Ron put out his hand and they shook. "You kids want to buy some bait?" he asked.

"No, but we have a question for you," Bradley said. "Do you know anyone with a black-and-white rabbit?" He handed Ron the pictures.

"Well, he's sitting in one of my boats, all right," Ron said. "But I've never seen the bunny before."

The kids told Ron about finding the rabbit in the closet at school. They explained that Douglas wouldn't eat and told him what the vet said.

Ron pulled on his nose. "I wish I could help," he said. "Have you tried asking at the pet shop on Main Street?"

"Yes, but they don't know the rabbit, either," Lucy said.

"Wait a second," Ron said. "My wife might have rented out the boat."

He pulled out a cell phone and punched in some numbers. "Honey, it's me at the shop. Do you remember renting one of the boats to a guy with a rabbit? You did? Who was it, do you remember? The Pinto twins and their friends are here trying to find the rabbit's owner."

Ron listened for another minute, then said good-bye. "My wife says it was an older man with white hair," he told the kids. "He rented the boat last summer."

"Did your wife write down his name?" Bradley asked. He had his fingers crossed.

Ron nodded his head. "Yep, we always take names when we rent boats," he said. "But it's tax time. We sent all our paperwork to our accountant. The slip of paper with his name on it is in a box with hundreds of others."

The kids thanked Ron Pinkowski and left. A cold wind blew off the river. A few small snowflakes flew into their faces.

Bradley felt his stomach sink. They were running out of clues and time. *Someone in this town has to know who owns Douglas,* he thought.

Then he realized there was a person in town who knew everyone!

"Come on, we're going to Ellie's

Diner!" Bradley yelled into the wind.

"I don't have any money," Nate said.

"We're going there to talk to Ellie," Bradley said. "She knows everyone, so maybe she knows rabbits, too!"

Cutting across the school grounds, it took them only a few minutes to reach the diner. The inside was warm and smelled like doughnuts. They sat in a booth by the window and took off their mittens.

"Hi, kids," Ellie said. She was wiping a shelf where she kept doughnuts, cookies, and bagels. She placed some cookies on a plate. "Here, eat these. They're left over. If you don't want them, I'll feed them to the squirrels."

The kids thanked Ellie and each took a cookie.

Bradley pulled out the pictures again. "This is Douglas. We're looking for his owner," he said. He explained how they had found Douglas at school the morning before.

"He misses his owner and won't eat," Bradley said.

"We think the owner is an older man with white hair," said Nate.

Ellie studied the pictures. "I've seen this rabbit," she said.

8
Ellie
to the Rescue

"You have? Where?" Bradley asked.

"Out front," Ellie told the excited kids. "It was around Thanksgiving, and it was real warm outside. A boy came by on a bike." Ellie tapped one of the pictures. "This rabbit was sitting in the bike's basket."

"Do you know who the boy was?" asked Nate.

Ellie shook her head. "No, I don't think he was from Green Lawn," she said. "He was older than you kids. He might have been visiting someone for the holiday."

"Maybe he was visiting the man with the scar on his finger!" Lucy said.

"It could be his grandfather," Brian suggested.

Bradley pulled out the picture that showed Douglas sitting on a lawn near a hedge. "And maybe this is that man's lawn," he said.

Ellie pointed toward the back of her diner. "When the boy left, he rode his bike that way, toward the bird streets," she said.

"What's a bird street?" asked Lucy.

"Over by Bridge Lane all the streets are named after birds," Brian explained.

The four kids huddled over the picture.

"There are at least ten bird streets," Brian said. "They all have lawns, and they all have hedges."

Bradley put his finger on the picture. "Look, there's something on the other side of that hedge," he said.

"It looks like a building," Lucy said.

"Guys, I think it's the town hall," Nate said. "That must be the flag on top."

"No, it can't be the town hall," Brian said. "There are no houses near it, and no hedges."

Bradley held the picture closer. "It's Center Church!" he said. "That isn't a flag on top, it's the church steeple."

Bradley looked up, grinning. "All we have to do is find which house has a view of the church over the hedge!" he said.

"Almost all of them do, Brad," Brian said. "We'll never find the right one."

"Yes, we will," Bradley said. He slipped the pictures into a pocket. "We have to, for Douglas!"

"So what do we do?" Nate asked.

"We should walk down Bridge Lane," Bradley suggested. "We'll pass by all the bird streets, and we can look over the hedges for the church."

The kids thanked Ellie and pulled on their mittens. Outside, the wind was blowing harder. The sky was dark gray.

"It's starting to snow," Nate said. He stuck his tongue out to catch a flake.

"Let's hurry!" Bradley said.

The kids walked past the fitness center and turned left onto Bridge Lane. The first street they came to was Wren Drive. They walked to the end of the short street, where tall hedges grew. They looked over the hedges.

"I can see the church," Bradley said. "But it doesn't look like the same view as in the picture."

"Let's try the next street," suggested Lucy.

They hurried back up Wren Drive, then went left to Blue Jay Way.

They peered over the hedge behind the last house. "This doesn't look right, either," Brian said.

They could all see the church steeple. But when they compared it to the picture, the views didn't seem the same.

They looked over the hedges behind Pheasant Lane, Owl Road, and Thrush Court. One of the hedges was too tall. Another one had a tree growing out of it. The hedge at the end of Thrush Court had a white fence in front of it.

"None of these are right," Bradley said.

"How many more of these bird streets are there?" Lucy asked.

"A few more," Bradley said. His nose was red and running. Snowflakes were catching in his eyelashes. "Come on, guys, it has to be one of these."

The kids hiked Finch Lane. They came to a small yellow house. Behind the house was a neat hedge. It was covered with snow.

Bradley pulled out the picture and held it up. "I think we found the street!" he said.

9
The Man
with the Scar

"Now what do we do?" Lucy asked.

"Let's knock on some doors," Nate suggested.

"Then what?" Brian asked. "We can't ask them if they left their rabbit in our closet."

"Why not?" Nate asked.

"Because whoever did it doesn't want us to know," Brian said.

Just then they noticed a man wearing a heavy coat and hat walking toward them. He was carrying a stack of flattened cardboard boxes.

"Hey, guys, that's Mr. Neater, the school janitor," Brian said.

"Hi, kids, enjoying your long weekend?" Mr. Neater asked. Snowflakes had covered his hat and shoulders.

"Hi, Mr. Neater," Lucy said. "Can we help you carry those?"

"I never refuse help," Mr. Neater said. "Here you go."

The kids took the empty boxes from Mr. Neater's arms. They followed him to the last house on Finch Lane. A FOR SALE sign stuck out of the snow in front. Bradley looked over the hedge and saw the church steeple.

"Are you selling your house, Mr. Neater?" Bradley asked.

He nodded. "Yep. Retiring in a couple of weeks," he said. "I'll be moving to a smaller place."

Mr. Neater climbed up his front steps. "Just dump those boxes here on the porch, please," he said.

He moved a wicker chair to make room.

That was when Bradley noticed the scar shaped like a *C* on Mr. Neater's pinkie finger.

10
Mystery Man

Bradley tried not to stare at the finger. He thought about the picture in his pocket. Did the scar on Mr. Neater's finger match the one in the photo? Bradley decided that they did match.

"We found Douglas," Bradley said.

Mr. Neater looked at Bradley. Then he sighed and sat in the chair. "And how is my furry friend?" he asked.

"We think he's sick!" Lucy said.

"We even took him to the vet!" Brian added.

"Dr. Henry told us Douglas needs you, Mr. Neater," Bradley said.

"You're the mystery man!" Nate said. "You left him in our classroom closet. You covered the cage with a towel that has a *Z* on it."

"Not a *Z*, son," Mr. Neater said. "You must have turned it sideways. It's an *N*, for *Neater.* How did you find me?"

Bradley showed him the three pictures. "We found clues in these," he said.

"Ah, yes," Mr. Neater said.

"He misses you," Brian said. "He won't eat, and we're afraid he'll die!"

"Douglas is at your house?" Mr. Neater asked.

"We brought him home for the long weekend," Bradley said. "But he won't eat or drink or play. He just sits there looking sad."

"Oh dear, I hadn't counted on that,"

Mr. Neater said. "Show me where you live."

The kids led Mr. Neater back up Bridge Lane and across Main Street.

They cut around the elementary school to Eagle Lane. From there they could see Bradley and Brian's house on Farm Lane.

The four kids burst through the kitchen door. The twins' mother was sitting at the table. She had Douglas in her lap, trying to feed him water from a baby bottle.

"Mom, this is Mr. Neater!" Bradley said. "He works at the school—"

"And he's Douglas's owner!" Brian cut in. "We found him!"

"Thank goodness!" the twins' mom said. "I've been trying to get Douglas to eat or drink, but he refuses."

"May I?" Mr. Neater got down on his knees. He took Douglas from Mrs.

Pinto. He held the rabbit and whispered into his ears. Suddenly Douglas opened his eyes. His ears shot straight up. He began rubbing his nose against Mr. Neater's coat.

"He recognizes you!" Lucy cried.

Mr. Neater smiled. "Of course he does," the man said. "I've had Douglas for nine years, since he was no bigger than a hamster."

Bradley's mother handed Mr. Neater the baby bottle. He touched Douglas's nose with the nipple, and the rabbit began to suck water into his mouth.

"Awesome!" Nate cried.

After Douglas was finished drinking, everyone moved to the living room. The kids sat on the floor with Douglas. They took turns rolling a tennis ball across the rug. Douglas hopped after the ball. Each time he caught up with the ball, he batted it with one of his feet.

"He seems to be very happy now," Bradley's mother said.

"Why did you leave him at the school?" Bradley asked. "Why not just take him with you when you move?"

"When I retire, I'll be living at elderly housing on Main Street," Mr. Neater said. "They don't allow pets, so I had to find him a new home. I saw what good care your class takes of your hamster and turtle, so I brought Douglas there."

"Mr. Vooray said our class might be able to keep him," Brian said. "But Douglas needs you!"

Mr. Neater looked sad. "It seems that Douglas and I have a problem," he said. "I can't take him, and I can't leave him."

11
Bradley's Dream

Bradley's mom offered Mr. Neater a ride home in her car.

Douglas's ears stood straight up when they put him back in his cage. His nose was twitching, and his eyes were bright.

"Look how happy he is," Bradley said.

"I can keep him for two more weeks," Mr. Neater said. "But I don't know what I'm going to do when I move."

Bradley remembered the boy with

the bike basket Ellie had mentioned. "Do you have a grandson?" he asked Mr. Neater.

"Yes, his name is Myron," Mr. Neater said. "He lives in Vermont."

"Could he take Douglas?" Bradley asked.

Mr. Neater shook his head. "I already thought of that. But Myron's mom is allergic," he said.

After Mr. Neater and Douglas left, the kids sat in a circle. They rolled the ball back and forth between them.

"We have to think of something," Bradley said.

"I have an idea," Brian said. "We can hypnotize Douglas into thinking Mr. Vooray is Mr. Neater."

The other three kids just looked at Brian.

"You can't hypnotize animals," Nate said.

"Who says?" Brian asked. "I saw on TV where these people put an alligator to sleep by rubbing its belly."

"But that's not hypnotizing," Lucy said. "Besides, rabbits are smarter than alligators. Douglas would know that Mr. Vooray isn't Mr. Neater!"

"Guys, we need a plan here," Bradley said.

No one could think of one.

That night, Bradley had a dream. In his dream, Douglas was playing in a big meadow of wildflowers. Hundreds of other rabbits were in the field with him. The rabbits chased each other and tumbled in the tall grass and flowers.

Bradley woke up the next morning with a plan. He woke his brother, then called Lucy and Nate.

After breakfast, Bradley and Brian walked down Main Street. They cut between the town hall and the Shangri-la

Hotel. Lucy and Nate were waiting for them at the town petting zoo.

"This is a great idea!" Lucy said. "Douglas can live here with the other animals. And Mr. Neater can visit him anytime!"

"That's what I thought," Bradley said. "They have other rabbits here, too."

The kids walked into the petting zoo office. A man with a friendly face was sitting at a desk. He wore a dark green shirt with a PETTING ZOO patch on the sleeve. "Can I help you?" he asked.

The kids walked over to the man's desk. Suddenly a little furry face peeked out of one of the desk drawers.

"Don't mind Slinky," the man said. "He's a ferret. Very sweet, very friendly."

The kids all petted Slinky.

"And my name is Barney," the man went on. "How can I help you?"

"We have a friend who has a pet rabbit," Bradley said. He told Barney about the problem Mr. Neater was having with Douglas. "Can Douglas come and live here?"

Barney shook his head. "I'm afraid we have a problem, too," he said. "We may have to shut down the petting zoo."

12
A Perfect Plan

"Why?" all four kids asked at once.

"There are three of us working here," Barney told the kids. "Brenda, Tom, and me. We feed the animals, make sure they get exercise, clean their cages, do just about everything. But I'm going back to college, and Brenda is getting married and moving away. That leaves just Tom, and he can't do everything by himself."

Barney picked up Slinky and set him on his shoulder. "We'll have to find

homes for all the animals if we close,"
he said. "I'm taking Slinky with me to
college."

Bradley thought about all the other
animals at the petting zoo. He'd been
coming here since he was a baby.

"So you see why we can't take your
friend's rabbit," Barney said. "We can't
even keep our own rabbits."

Just then Barney's telephone rang.
He waved good-bye to the kids and
answered the phone.

The kids walked outside. They cut
between the town hall and the library to
West Green Street.

"Is this where Mr. Neater will be living?" Lucy asked. She pointed to the
building next to the police station.

"Yeah, and it's a nice place," Bradley
said.

"Our mom volunteers there once a
week," Brian added. "She helps the

people do art projects and stuff."

"Oh my gosh, I've got it!" Bradley cried.

"Got what?" his brother asked.

"A new plan, but first we have to go see Mr. Neater again."

Bradley explained his idea on the way.

Five minutes later, they knocked on Mr. Neater's front door.

Mr. Neater answered. He was holding Douglas in his arms.

"Well, hello again," the man said. "Come in out of the cold."

The kids piled their coats on a chair.

"We have an idea about Douglas," Bradley said.

Mr. Neater was stroking Douglas's long, silky ears. "Please tell us. We're all ears," he said with a grin.

The kids told Mr. Neater about their visit to the petting zoo. They explained what Barney told them about the place maybe having to close down.

"Douglas might love living there," Mr. Neater said. "But if they're going to shut down . . ."

"They wouldn't have to shut down if they had more people to take care of the animals," Lucy put in.

"We thought you could volunteer there after you retire from the school," Bradley said.

"That way you could see Douglas every day, and he wouldn't feel lonely!" Nate added.

Mr. Neater stared at the four kids. "Volunteering at the petting zoo might be fun," he said after a minute. "And it's only a few minutes' walk from elderly housing."

"You'll do it?" Bradley cried.

Mr. Neater smiled. "If it's okay with Douglas, it's okay with me!"

. . .

Douglas went to live at the petting zoo.
Mr. Neater moved into elderly housing
and began volunteering at the zoo. He
saw his rabbit every day.

One Saturday the kids decided to
pay Mr. Neater a visit at the zoo. What a
surprise they got when they walked into
the warm animal building.

Bradley saw at least ten elderly people wearing dark green shirts. One man
was brushing a small goat. A woman
was placing fresh straw in cages. Two
men were washing the floor with a garden hose.

Mr. Neater walked over to the kids.
He was holding Douglas. "Hey, kids," he
said.

"Hi, Mr. Neater!" the kids said.

"Who are all these people?" Bradley
asked.

"They're all volunteers from elderly

housing," Mr. Neater said. "I got them to agree to help out here at the zoo. They love the animals, and the animals get a lot more care and attention."

A woman with white hair walked by with a bag of corn in her hand. A white duck followed her, quacking loudly.

Bradley smiled. His plan had worked. "Can I hold Douglas?" he asked.

Mr. Neater placed Douglas in Bradley's arms. The rabbit sniffed Bradley's sweater. Then he closed his eyes and snuggled into the soft wool.

If you like Calendar Mysteries, you might want to read A to Z Mysteries!

Help Dink, Josh, and Ruth Rose . . .

. . . solve mysteries from A to Z!

STEPPING STONES

Track down all these books for a little mystery in your life!

A to Z Mysteries®
by Ron Roy

Calendar Mysteries
by Ron Roy

Capital Mysteries
by Ron Roy

Marion Dane Bauer
The Blue Ghost
The Green Ghost
The Red Ghost
The Secret of the Painted House

Polly Berrien Berends
The Case of the Elevator Duck

Éric Sanvoisin
The Ink Drinker

George Edward Stanley
Ghost Horse

Read all of KC and Marshall's adventures in Washington, D.C.!

Capital Mysteries